I Can Read!™

ZONDERkidz

Otter and Owl Say I'm Sorry

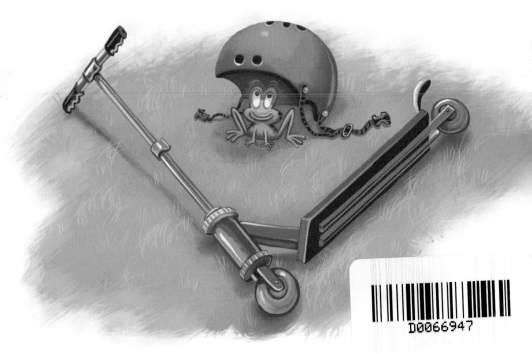

story by Crystal Bowman

pictures by Kevin Zimmer

Owl sat on a rock by the pond.

His friend Otter rode by.

Otter was riding a new scooter.

"Whose scooter is that?" asked Owl.

"It's mine," said Otter.

"It goes very fast."

"May I ride it?" asked Owl.

"Okay," said Otter.

Owl rode the scooter back and forth.

He rode it around and around.

Then Owl stopped.

"I've been thinking," said Owl.

"The scooter will go much faster

if we ride it down the hill."

Otter and Owl pushed the scooter

to the top of the hill.

Otter got on the scooter behind Owl.

"Here we go!" said Otter.

"Hold on tight!" said Owl.

The scooter sped down the hill

faster and faster and faster.

"Yippee!" said Otter.

"Yippee!" said Owl.

The scooter was headed for the pond.

"Turn the wheel!" cried Otter.

But it was too late.

Crash!

They landed in the pond.

"I'm all wet!" said Owl.

"Me too," said Otter.

"And so is my scooter!"

They pulled it out of the pond.

"We can dry it off," said Owl.

Owl helped Otter dry his scooter.

"Oh no!" cried Otter.

"The wheel is broken!"

Owl looked at the wheel.

It pointed the wrong way.

"Maybe we can fix it," said Owl.

Otter and Owl tried to fix the wheel.

It was no use.

"You broke my scooter!" said Otter.

"What kind of friend does that?"

Otter went home.

Owl went home too.

"I am a bad friend," he thought.

"I'm the worst friend in the world."

Owl did not feel like eating dinner.

Then Owl had an idea.

He got his paper and crayons.

He wrote a note to Otter.

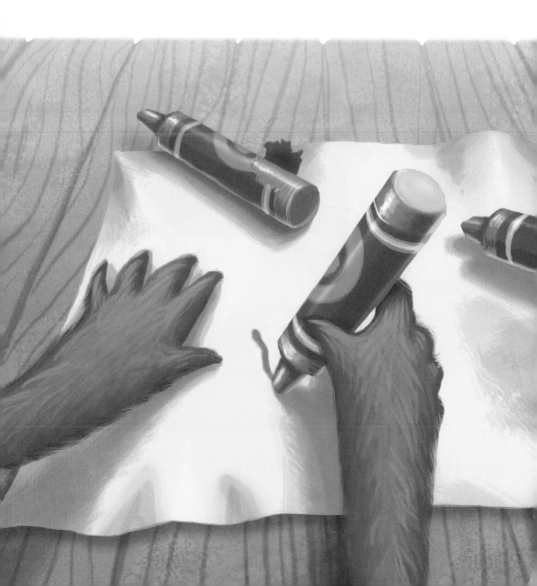

Owl went to Otter's house.

He put the note on the step.

He knocked on the door and ran away.

Otter opened the door.

He didn't see anyone

so he shut the door.

Otter heard another knock

on the door.

Otter opened the door again.

He did not see anyone there.

But this time he saw the note.

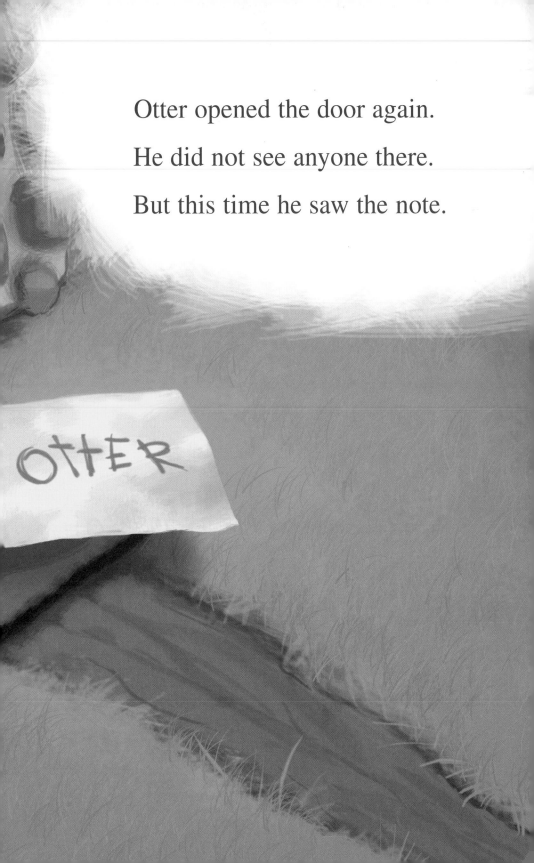

Otter picked up the note and read it.

Dear Otter,

I am so sorry.
Please forgive me.
You may have all
my toys and my
very best hat.

I want to be
friends again.

Love, Owl.

Otter took the note inside.

Soon there was a knock on the door.

It was Owl.

"Will you forgive me?" he asked.

Otter nodded his head.

"I will forgive you," he said.

"God wants friends to forgive

each other."

Owl smiled a big smile.

"Do you want some pizza?"

asked Otter.

"Oh yes!" said Owl. "I'm hungry!"

They closed their eyes to pray.

"Thank you for pizza," said Otter.

"Thank you for friends," said Owl.

The next day Otter went to Owl's house.

"Do you want all my toys

and my very best hat?" asked Owl.

"No," said Otter.

"I want to take you for a ride
on my scooter," said Otter.

"Your scooter is broken," said Owl.

"I fixed it," said Otter.

Otter and Owl hopped on the scooter.

The scooter did not go very fast.

It even wobbled back and forth.

But Otter and Owl had fun anyway.

Dear Parent:
Your child's love of reading starts here!

Every child learns to read in a different way and at his or her own speed. You can help your young reader improve and become more confident by encouraging his or her own interests and abilities. You can also guide your child's spiritual development by reading stories with biblical values and Bible stories, like I Can Read! books published by Zonderkidz. From books your child reads with you to the first books he or she reads alone, there are I Can Read! books for every stage of reading:

SHARED READING
Basic language, word repetition, and whimsical illustrations, ideal for sharing with your emergent reader.

BEGINNING READING
Short sentences, familiar words, and simple concepts for children eager to read on their own.

READING WITH HELP
Engaging stories, longer sentences, and language play for developing readers.

READING ALONE
Complex plots, challenging vocabulary, and high-interest topics for the independent reader.

ADVANCED READING
Short paragraphs, chapters, and exciting themes for the perfect bridge to chapter books.

I Can Read! books have introduced children to the joy of reading since 1957. Featuring award-winning authors and illustrators and a fabulous cast of beloved characters, I Can Read! books set the standard for beginning readers.

A lifetime of discovery begins with the magical words **"I Can Read!"**

Visit www.icanread.com for information on enriching your child's reading experience.
Visit www.zonderkidz.com for more Zonderkidz I Can Read! titles.

Be kind and tender to one another.
Forgive each other, just as God forgave you
because of what Christ has done.
—*Ephesians 4:32*

.·:

Otter and Owl Say I'm Sorry
Copyright © 2008 by Crystal Bowman
Illustrations copyright © 2008 by Kevin Zimmer

Requests for information should be addressed to:
Zonderkidz, Grand Rapids, Michigan 49530

Library of Congress Cataloging-in-Publication Data:

Bowman, Crystal.
  Otter and Owl say I'm sorry / by Crystal Bowman ; illustrated by Kevin Zimmer.
    p. cm. – (I can read. Level 1)
  ISBN 978-0-310-71707-2 (softcover : alk. paper) [1. Friendship–Fiction. 2. Forgiveness–
Fiction. 3. Christian life–Fiction.] I. Zimmer, Kevin, ill. II. Title. III. Title: Otter and Owl say I
am sorry.
  PZ7.B6834Ow 2008
  [E]--dc22
                                                          2008009582

Art Direction and Design: Jody Langley

Printed in China

08 09 10 • 4 3 2 1